Y0-ECU-598

my itty-bitty bio

Laura Bush

CHERRY LAKE PRESS

Published in the United States of America by Cherry Lake Publishing Group
Ann Arbor, Michigan
www.cherrylakepublishing.com

Reading Adviser: Marla Conn, MS Ed., Literacy specialist, Read-Ability, Inc.
Book Designer: Jennifer Wahi
Illustrator: Jeff Bane

Photo Credits: ©G B Hart/shutterstock, 5; ©Cheryl Casey/shutterstock, 7; ©connel/shutterstock, 9; ©National Archives Catalog/ARC ID 75597831, 11; ©Joseph Sohm/shutterstock, 13, 22; ©Public Domain/White House photo/Photograph by Paul Morse, 15, 23; ©National Archives Catalog/ARC ID 78086792, 17; ©National Archives Catalog/ARC ID 171487157, 19; ©National Archives Catalog/ARC ID 172544096, 21; Jeff Bane, Cover, 1, 8, 12,16

Copyright ©2021 by Cherry Lake Publishing Group
All rights reserved. No part of this book may be reproduced or utilized in any form or by any means without written permission from the publisher.

Cherry Lake Press is an imprint of Cherry Lake Publishing Group.

Library of Congress Cataloging-in-Publication Data

Names: Pincus, Meeg, author. | Bane, Jeff, 1957- illustrator.
Title: Laura Bush / Meeg Pincus ; illustrated by Jeff Bane.
Description: Ann Arbor, Michigan : Cherry Lake Publishing, 2021. | Series: My itty-bitty bio | Includes index. | Audience: Grades K-1 | Summary: "The My Itty-Bitty Bio series are biographies for the earliest readers. This book examines the life of former First Lady Laura Bush in a simple, age-appropriate way that will help young readers develop word recognition and reading skills. Includes a table of contents, author biography, timeline, glossary, index, and other informative backmatter"-- Provided by publisher.
Identifiers: LCCN 2020035870 (print) | LCCN 2020035871 (ebook) | ISBN 9781534179981 (hardcover) | ISBN 9781534181694 (paperback) | ISBN 9781534180994 (pdf) | ISBN 9781534182707 (ebook)
Subjects: LCSH: Bush, Laura Welch, 1946- --Juvenile literature. | Presidents' spouses--United States--Biography--Juvenile literature.
Classification: LCC E904.B87 P56 2021 (print) | LCC E904.B87 (ebook) | DDC 973.931092 [B]--dc23
LC record available at https://lccn.loc.gov/2020035870
LC ebook record available at https://lccn.loc.gov/2020035871

Printed in the United States of America
Corporate Graphics

table of contents

My Story 4

Timeline 22

Glossary 24

Index 24

About the author: Meeg Pincus has been a writer, editor, and educator for 25 years. She loves to write inspiring stories for kids about people, animals, and our planet. She lives near San Diego, California, where she enjoys the beach, reading, singing, and her family.

About the illustrator: Jeff Bane and his two business partners own a studio along the American River in Folsom, California, home of the 1849 Gold Rush. When Jeff's not sketching or illustrating for clients, he's either swimming or kayaking in the river to relax.

my story

I was born in Texas. It was 1946.

I was an only child. My parents **valued** learning. I loved to read books.

What books do you like to read?

I went to college in Texas.
I became a teacher and librarian.

I married George W. Bush.
We had twin daughters.

I helped my husband become the **governor** of Texas. I raised money for Texas libraries and preschools.

My husband became president of the United States. This meant I became the **First Lady**. Our family moved to Washington, D.C.

I helped pass education laws. I helped teachers. I started a huge book **festival**.

I have traveled around the world.
I helped with health education.
I worked with women and children.
I spoke up for **human rights**.

Where would you like to travel?

I am **devoted** to education and reading. I have helped children, families, and adults around the world.

What would you like to ask me?

timeline

1995

1940

↑
Born
1946

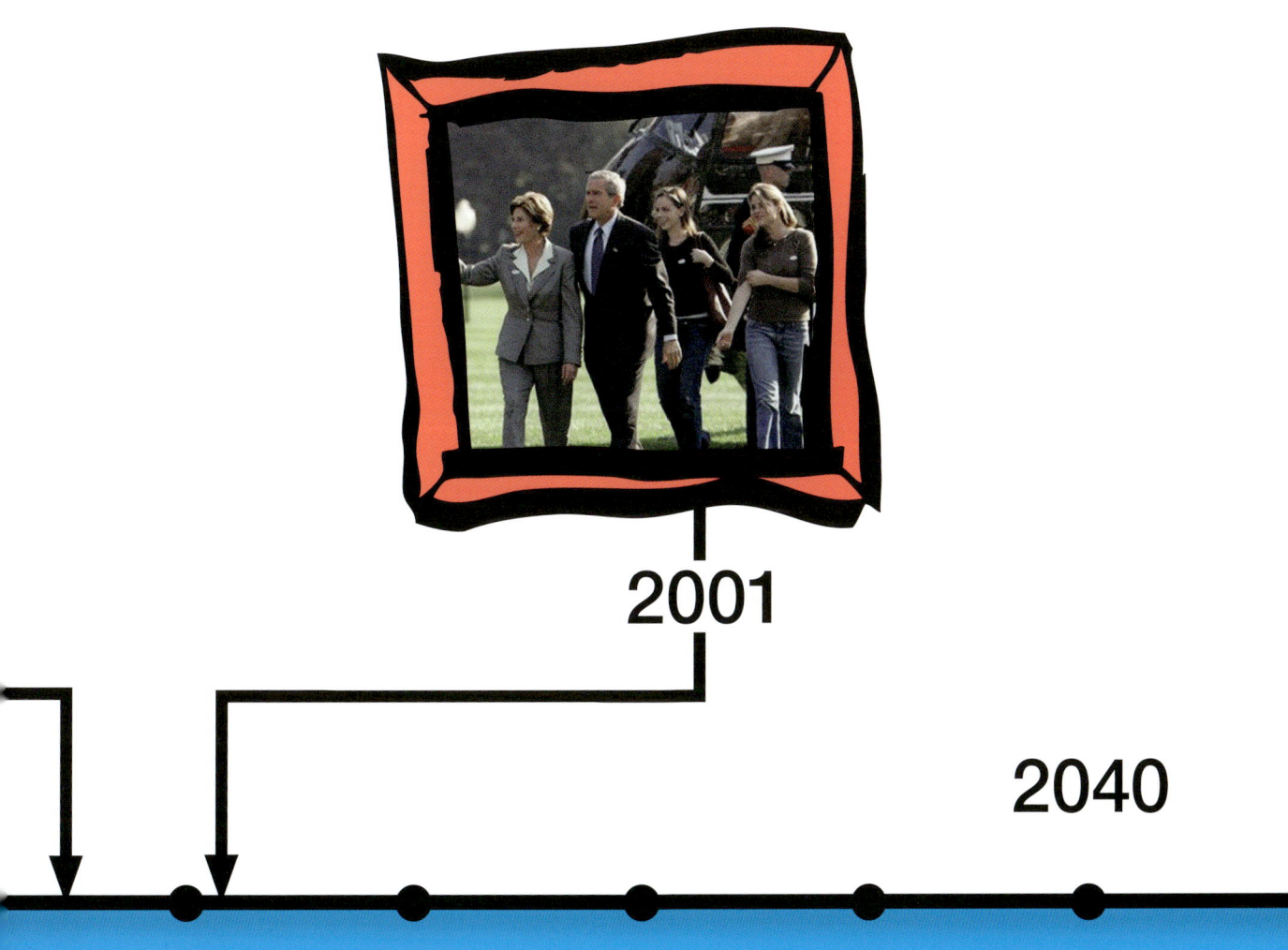

2001

2040

glossary & index

glossary

devoted (dih-VOH-tid) having or showing strong feelings of faithfulness and love

festival (FES-tuh-vuhl) a yearly event that honors something, such as arts or music

First Lady (FURST LAY-dee) the wife of the president of the United States

governor (GUHV-ur-nur) the highest elected official of a U.S. state

human rights (HYOO-muhn RITES) everyone's right to justice, fair treatment, and free speech

valued (VAL-yood) to have thought something is important or loved

index

books, 6, 7, 16

education, 16, 18, 20

First Lady, 14

George W. Bush, 10
governor, 12

health, 18
human rights, 18

librarian, 8

read, 6, 7, 20

teacher, 8, 16
Texas, 4, 8, 12
travel, 18, 19
twin, 10